A Lion in the Meadow

D0334122

There are lots of Early Reader
stories you might enjoy.
Look at the back of the book
or, for a complete list, visit
www.orionbooks.co.uk

A Lion in the Meadow

Margaret Mahy

Illustrated by Jenny Williams

Orion
Children's Books

A Lion in the Meadow was originally published in 1969
by J.M. Dent & Sons
This edition first published in Great Britain in 2013
by Orion Children's Books
a division of the Orion Publishing Group Ltd
Orion House
5 Upper Saint Martin's Lane
London WC2H 9EA
An Hachette UK Company
3 5 7 9 10 8 6 4 2

Text © Margaret Mahy 1969, 1986
Illustrations © Jenny Williams 1986
The right of Margaret Mahy and Jenny Williams to be identified
as author and illustrator of this work has been asserted.

All rights reserved.
No part of this publication may be reproduced,
stored in a retrieval system, or transmitted, in any form
or by any means, electronic, mechanical, photocopying,
recording, or otherwise, without the prior permission
of Orion Children's Books.

The Orion Publishing Group's policy is to use papers
that are natural, renewable and recyclable products
and made from wood grown in sustainable forests.
The logging and manufacturing processes are expected
to conform to the environmental regulations
of the country of origin.

A catalogue record for this book is available
from the British Library.

ISBN 978 1 4440 0926 2

Printed and bound in China
www.orionbooks.co.uk

For Helen Hoke Watts
Margaret Mahy

For my children, Rowan and Bonnie
Jenny Williams

The little boy said, "Mother, there is a lion in the meadow."

The mother said,
"Nonsense, little boy."

The little boy said, "Mother,
there is a big, yellow lion in
the meadow."

The mother said, "Nonsense,
little boy."

The little boy said, "Mother,
there is a big, roaring, yellow,
whiskery lion in the meadow!"

The mother said, "Little boy,
you are making up stories again.
There is nothing in the meadow
but grass and trees. Go into the
meadow and see for yourself."

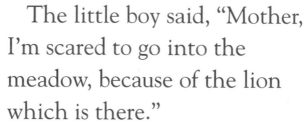

The little boy said, "Mother, I'm scared to go into the meadow, because of the lion which is there."

The mother said, "Little boy, you are making up stories – so I will make up a story, too…

Do you see this matchbox?

Take it out into the meadow
and open it. In it will be a tiny
dragon.

The tiny dragon will grow into
a big dragon. It will chase the
lion away."

The little boy took the
matchbox and went away.

The mother went on peeling
the potatoes.

Suddenly the door opened.
 In rushed a big, roaring, yellow,
whiskery lion.

"Hide me!" it
said. "A dragon
is after me!"

The lion hid
in the broom
cupboard.

Then the little boy came
running in.

"Mother," he said. "That
dragon grew too big. There is no
lion in the meadow now.

There is a dragon in the
meadow."

The little
boy hid in
the broom
cupboard
too.

"You should have
left me alone," said
the lion. "I eat
only apples."

"But there wasn't a real dragon," said the mother. "It was just a story I made up."

"It turned out to be true after all," said the little boy. "You should have looked in the matchbox first."

"That is how it is," said
the lion.

"Some stories are true and
some aren't...

But I have an idea. We will go and play in the meadow on the other side of the house.

There is no dragon there."

"I am glad we are friends now,"
said the little boy.

The little boy and the big, roaring, yellow, whiskery lion went to play in the other meadow.

The dragon stayed where he was, and nobody minded.

So the lion in the meadow
became a house lion and lived
in the broom cupboard.

And when the little boy had apples, stories and a goodnight hug, the lion had apples, stories and a goodnight hug as well.

Did you enjoy the story
of the lion in the meadow?

Can you roar like a lion?

Do you like apples too?

Can you draw a lion?

Can you draw a dragon?

Who are your friends?

Do you like goodnight hugs?

What are you going to read next?

More adventures with

or go to
sea with

Horrid Henry,

or into space with

Poppy the Pirate Dog,

You could
have fun
on

Cudweed.

A Rainbow Shopping Day,

or explore

Down in the Jungle,

but watch out for

A Creepy Crawly Story!

Make magic with

The Three Little Witches,

and have
a ball
with

Princesses.

Or follow the star in

The First Christmas.

Enjoy all the Early Readers.

Sign up for **the orion star** newsletter
for all the latest children's book news,
plus activity sheets, exclusive competitions,
author interviews, pre-publication extracts
and more.

www.orionbooks.co.uk/newsletters

Follow  @the_orionstar on .